Single
& Waiting

Dr. Lawrence

Single & Waiting

Dr. Jacqueline Lawrence

BET Publications, LLC
http://www.bet.com

NEW SPIRIT BOOKS are published by

BET Publications, LLC
c/o BET BOOKS
One BET Plaza
1900 W Place NE
Washington, DC 20018-1211

All Kensington Titles, Imprints, and Distributed Lines are available at special quantity discounts for bulk purchases for sales promotions, premiums, fund-raising, and educational or institutional use. Special book excerpts or customized printings can also be created to fit specific needs. For details, write or phone the office of the Kensington special sales manager: Kensington Publishing Corp., 850 Third Avenue, New York, NY 10022, attn: Special Sales Department, Phone: 1-800-221-2647.

Library of Congress Card Catalogue Number: 2004101674
ISBN: 1-58314-463-3

First Printing: September 2004
10 9 8 7 6 5 4 3 2 1

Printed in the United States of America

Special thanks to:

- *My Lord and Savior, Jesus Christ, who has loved me unconditionally, from the beginning of time, and has never once let me down.*

- *My beautiful daughters, Desireé Nicole and Alyssa Monét, who continue to stand by me in all that I do and all that I endure.*

- *My loving family who always keeps a space in their hearts open for me.*

- *The men and women who influenced the writing of the poems contained in this collection.*

- *My dear husband . . . for whom I am waiting.*

Contents

"Likewise, teach the older women to be reverent in the way they live, not to be slanderers or addicted to much wine, but to teach what is good. Then they can train the younger women to love their husbands and children to be self-controlled and pure, to be busy at home, to be kind, and to be subject to their husbands, so that no one will malign the word of God." (Titus 2:3–5)

"Teach the older men to be temperate, worthy of respect, self-controlled, and sound in faith, in love, and in endurance. Similarly, encourage the young men to be self-controlled. In everything set an example by doing what is good. In your teaching show integrity, seriousness and soundness of speech that cannot be condemned…" (Titus 2:2,6a)

Introduction

Greetings,

I am here to share with you some of my struggles with being a single, African-American, Christian sista in today's society. If you are single, have ever been single, or are planning on being single, I'm sure you will find something within these pages to which you can relate. I hope yawl don't mind the fact that my communication style is to keep it real with folks, so if my reality offends anyone, then charge it to my head and not my heart. . . . Amen?

If you, yourself, are not single, then I'm sure you know a whole lot of folks who are; or at least folks who need to be. I know that I'm not alone when I say that being single can sometimes feel isolating, lonely, empty, and perhaps even purposeless. Many of us single folks were raised to believe that we *need* a life's partner to make us complete. What we *need*, however, is to have a personal relationship with the Lord, Jesus Christ, who wants to give us the desires of our heart and fulfill our *every* need, as only *He* is willing and able to do so (Psalm 37:4, Philippians 4:19).

In order for us to be a suitable helpmate for someone else, we should first make sure that we are a full, whole, and complete person ourselves. We should be able to see ourselves as a cake—having all the ingredients necessary to make us firm and sweet. We shouldn't *"need"* a life's partner for that. However, a life's partner should be looked upon as the icing on our cake—simply adding more flavor and sweetness to our already whole and complete lives. Our lives would be blessed beyond measure, if we would only look to God for our provisions, our strength, our comfort . . . our everything, whether we are single or married. But too many times, we look to ourselves, other folks, finances, power, position, drugs, alcohol, material possessions, and other things to try and get our needs fulfilled.

We are all basically looking for the same thing in a relationship—unfailing love. We all want someone to give us love, and someone with whom we can share our love, without sacrificing our values and principles. We need to take everything we do very seriously (including selecting a mate) and not be willing to settle for anyone who is not worthy of being in our lives, because every decision we make—good and bad—affects our lives, the lives of one another, and most importantly, the lives of our children, our future. Therefore, it is not advantageous for us to yoke ourselves with non-believers, as our values have no commonality with them (2 Corinthians 6:14).

Most if not all the strife and setbacks that have come my way have been a result of *my* disobedience, *my* going against God's will for my life, and *my* yoking *myself* together with folks who were not worthy of being a part of my life. I could no longer be angry with them for all the anguish that they put me through, but had to look at myself and the reasons why I allowed them in my life. I was lonely, desperate, afraid to face myself, and had low self-esteem.

One day, while sitting in my lonely apartment, I pulled out a mirror and took a good, hard look at myself. I could see a glimmer of somebody looking back at me. That somebody was my soul. I pondered the reason why I had been neglecting her, putting everyone else first. It seemed as though the harder I looked at her, the more she tried to run away from me. As she crept back toward me with deep suspicion, she looked at me intently, wondering if she could trust me to take care of her, to love and to protect her. There we were, staring at one another, face to face, eye to eye. It was wonderful and comforting to finally make her acquaintance. She was beautiful, inside and out. She smiled at me, and I smiled back. My eyes filled with tears. They streamed down my face and onto the carpet. Then I slowly pulled out a pen and pad, and, trying hard not to release my gaze from her for fear that she may disappear, I wrote:

4

Somebody Has Been Wanting to Come Out

Somebody has been wanting to come out—somebody deep inside of me.
This somebody has dreams and ambitions deep inside of her.
I can tell that she wants to be set free, but why is she afraid of revealing herself to me?
"I can see you, you can come out. You're beautiful. I love you.
I want to be your best friend.
I will protect you from any harmful and hurtful thing that comes your way.
You can trust me. I promise. You've no more inhibitions, only yourself to answer to.
So bloom, blossom in every good way . . . Come out, come out!"

Looking around my apartment, I realized at that point, that my world (our world) is like a room with a door, and I didn't *have* to let everyone in. I am blessed that my door is equipped with a peep hole, a screen door, a deadbolt, a doorknob and a key; my peep hole, so I can look out to see who's standing on the other side of my door to determine if I even want to open it; my screen door, so that even if I *think* I want to open my door, I still have a safety net, and either I don't have to, or don't want to; my deadbolt, so that I can lock those out who are not worthy of coming inside; my doorknob, to open my door if I do meet someone who seems as though he might be worthy of coming inside; and lastly, my key, to be given only to a person, or persons, whom I trust enough to put my very life into their hands. I will not go around giving everybody my key.

When I started to look to God for answers, understanding, wisdom, love, patience, direction, and every other perfect thing, not allowing folks to treat me no any kind of way, my life became much more peaceful and my trials and tribulations decreased significantly in both frequency and intensity. My aim is to share with you some of my personal struggles with being a single, Christian, African-American sista, in hopes that your life will be spiritually enriched and glorified.

Although a few single people were blessed with the gift of being content with their singleness, most of us, I believe, would prefer to have a life partner—someone with whom we can go through the ups and downs in life. Relationships, however, require work, commitment, patience, understanding, and sacrifice. Marriage may look good on the outside, but no marriage or relationship is always a bed of roses. When a couple is walking in unity with the Lord, for better or worse, in sickness and in health, and for richer or poorer, till death do they part, then that is what a true marriage is all about.

I did go down that road a couple of times, albeit not for the right reasons. I figured from the start, that if things didn't work out, I could always get divorced. When I was sending out wedding invitations for my second wedding, I tried to remain numb because, on the outside, it was written, "Marriage is the union of two souls." I knew my soul was not united with that of my fiancé's, yet, I hurriedly stuffed the envelopes, trying my best to remain stiff with denial about the big mistake I was about to make. While walking down the aisle during my wedding ceremony, I actually said the word "help" in hopes that someone would deliver me from making such a huge mistake. Still, I continued with my walk, my knees shaking so much I thought I would collapse. When I finally made it up to the front, I had my personal vows in my hand because I was planning on reading them. I knew I had nothing to say from my heart but lies. The paper was too sweaty and I could not read it, so I had to improvise. I didn't know what to say, but whatever I said, I refused to tell the lie that I loved him. I can't tell you all how bad I felt lying to myself, my soon-to-be husband, the other witnesses, and most importantly, to God.

I now understand that marriage is nothing to play with! It was ordained by God to be holy and sacred. When we play with marriage, we're playing with God, and there will be consequences for playing with God!

Although most of us would rather have someone around with whom we can share our lives, singleness also has its rewards: we have no one whom to answer. We can come and go as we please; go to bed smelling as funky as we want; spend our money on whatever we choose; parent our children our way; and eat cereal for breakfast, lunch, and dinner seven nights a week, if we so choose, without having to explain or defend ourselves to anyone. I try to embrace the benefits of being single because, at this time in my life, that is what God has for me, so I might as well make the best of it!

Although there are struggles associated with being single, God allows, and even admires singleness (1 Corinthians 7:1). In 1 Corinthians 7:7, Paul even refers to the ability of being single as a gift from God. Contrary to popular belief, Paul states that people who are married, and not those who are single, will face many troubles (1 Corinthians 7:28). He further warns that it is best to be single because, as single folks, our devotion is to the Lord; but when we get married, we are devoted to pleasing our spouses. Thus our interests are divided. Therefore, if it is possible for us to do so, it is better that we remain single so that we may live in a right way, in individual devotion to the Lord. Jesus tells us, in fact, that at the Resurrection, we will all be single (Matthew 22:30).

The world looks upon being single as somewhat of a negative thing; single folks pay higher taxes and insurance, get fewer employee benefits, receive smaller social security benefits, and are looked on as being unworthy of being in a relationship, unstable, lonely, and desperate for a mate. But through the eyes of the Lord, being single is a good thing. If we were all single in this world, as the Lord truly desires for us to be, then our concern would be about how we can please Him (1 Corinthians 7:32). God's desire is for us to settle the matter of being single in our minds, but many are unsettled with their singleness and spend too much of their time trying to find the right mate, and too little time trying to be in a right devotion with God.

There was a time when I spent a lot of my energy focusing on having a husband, but that was time wasted. Life went on, and I am still single, and will be, until the time that God says otherwise, if it is His will to say. In the meantime, He has given me time and space in my life to do good works for Him, and to grow spiritually, and I have gotten to the point where I am thankful for the opportunity. Instead of directing my focus upon a man, I have decided to focus my attention on learning the valuable lessons that the Lord teaches me, so that I can be the best person that I can be for His sake. To me, this is both exciting and fulfilling! Racking my brain about when I was going to get my husband, and wondering, with each man I met, "Is he the one for me?" only wore me out and made me tired.

I'm Tired

I've spent so much time thinking about men;
time I could have spent on myself
developing my own worth, but instead,
I put some of me on a shelf
to come back to
when there was nothing left for me to do.

All that fantasizing about married life
has left me high and dry.
I'm back to where I started out,
so why should I even try
to find a love to call my own,
when I should be trying to deal with being alone?

As long as I can remember, I've asked the good Lord
to send somebody my way.

Sure, men have come and then they left.
Why can't somebody love me and stay?

I happen to know something they must not know,
and that is: I'm a heck of a woman.

Perhaps I'm too good for most guys and that's why
so many have swallowed their pride and ran.

I ain't gonna stress myself out, trying to figure it out.
God knows what I need.
He's heard me plead.
I'm tired—tired of searching, tired of being fired-up
when I meet somebody new.
I'm tired—tired of working at looking good.
What good does it do?

If they want me, I'm here. I ain't goin' nowhere.
Just gonna keep on sayin' my prayers—
'cause I'm tired.

Sometimes, in my complacency, I wonder if I even want a man in my life. After all, being single isn't so bad.

Through

I don't think I want a man. I'm leaving them alone.
Ain't gonna settle, just gonna flow all on my own.
I'm sick and tired of the mess, can't find anyone that's true.
I'll give myself some happiness, since I can't find any in you.

Thanks for driving me to this.
Now I can just sit back and chill.
What I never had I cannot miss,
but what I have, it has to be real.

I'm throwing in the towel, girlfriends;
getting out of the game.
These things that call themselves men,
I refuse to lower my pride and claim.
So go ahead, take your pick, choose from
whatever's left behind.
You can even have my leftovers . . . I promise, I won't mind.

Why would a man be single these days
with all these single women around?
Perhaps they've been snugly tucked away
in somebody's "lost and found."
I don't need to make myself feel good

by sitting around bashing men,
but based on my personal experience,
something just ain't right with some of them.

Until one of them comes along and proves that I am wrong,
I'm gonna stick to my guns and keep on
singing this same old hopeless song,
'cause I'm tired.

Some of the areas that have been a struggle for me as a single, Christian, African-American sista are men, waiting on the Lord, abstinence, black men going to white women, and the lack of love among man in our society today. I have come to share how the Lord has helped me to overcome these struggles and hope that, through my experiences, your lives can be enriched.

Single Sistas

Throughout my walk in life, I have acquainted myself with many single sistas. Some, like myself, are strong and independent, doing their *own* thing, regardless of the fact that they do *not* have husbands. They have their *own* places, their *own* jobs, their *own* money, their *own* cars, and many are taking care of their *own* children by their *own* selves.

Why Do I Have To Be In Need?

I've worked hard to become the independent woman
that I happen to be.
Somehow my independence gets mistaken
for my not wanting anything for free—
like the goodies some women get—
just because I'm able to get them on my own.
I shouldn't have to be in need, poor, desperate,
or broke down to the bone
just to get a little something—something
like the ladies with the sad stories do.
Why do I have to be in need to feel
like I'm being appreciated, too?
I have just as much to offer (if not more)
than those women who "get over" on men.
Why must I be punished just because I don't beg, whine,
*   scheme, and connive when*
I want something done special for me that makes me feel good,
like getting my nails done,
eating at a restaurant,
seeing a play,
getting my car fixed,
or just having fun?
I really don't feel that I should have to

ask to have something done for me.
It seems to me that if a man were interested,
he would want to see me pleased.
Even the bible talks about where a man's heart is,
there shall his treasure lie,
so if a man really cared for me,
he would want to do for me regardless of my
circumstances:
whether I may happen to be in need,
or even if I am not.
Just don't assume that I don't want or deserve anything
based on what I've got.

50-50

What's going on these days?
Doesn't a man know a real woman when he sees one?
Planning a date like a business proposition;
that takes out all the fun.

Where did the notion come from,
that everything should be 50-50?
Why should I have to go in half?
Don't you think I'm worth a simple dinner?
Your weakness makes me want to laugh!

If I'm doing 50, why do I need you?
Might as well be by myself, and you should, too.
What if I needed more than 50 from you?
Suppose I wanted to give you more, then what am I to do?

50-50 is a gridlock, a stalemate.
Nobody gives, nobody receives.
Nobody wins, nobody loses.
What a tangled web we weave.

Tell me, what are you afraid of, little boy?
Are you afraid you'll come out short?

There's more to a relationship than merely finances.
These days, men don't want to take time to court.

You want me to start out acting like your wife;
cook your meals, drive my car and invite you into my bed.
You don't want to do a thing for me;
It must be true that chivalry is dead.

If I can't be treated like the lady that I am,
I'll keep on spending time alone.
I'll keep on treating myself like I'm special.
I'll keep on being on my own.

I'll keep on buying my own dinner (thank you).
You keep your 50, I'll keep mine.
One day I'll meet up with a real man—I know it—
Who can appreciate a woman of my kind.

Most, if not all of the single sistas I know, however, have one thing in common—they want a single brotha; not just any single brotha, but many only want the one who they have conjured up in their *own* mind as being the "perfect" man for them. They tend to know exactly what it is that they want, or at least what qualities that they don't want, and won't accept, in a man. He has to have a job, his own place, a nice ride, and wear a suit and tie to work. He must be willing to spend money on them and their children, do the "man things" around the house, as well as at least half of the "woman things," and he'd better make more money than them, pay their bills, and get their hair and nails done on a regular basis, if he expects them to look good for him. He can't have a single blemish on his credit report. Nor can he have any children, but if he does, it can't be more than one. If it is, he'd better not have more than one baby's mama. And by all means he has to be tall and fine and not too black or not too light. And when we find him, or when we think we have found him, we know that we can't show too much interest, but our job is to make him want us. Yawl know how we do it.

Tiptoe Lightly

We've got to tiptoe lightly, ladies,
don't call them every time you want to;
wait till they call you.
Certainly don't make any popcorn visits.
Wait for them to offer you their digits.
Purposely forget some of the things they say.
If you hold on to everything, it'll run them away.

We've got to tiptoe lightly, ladies,
wouldn't want them to think we're too interested;
makes us look desperate.
Then they surely won't want us, but will run away.
If we want them to stay,
we've got to sneak up on them and act like we don't care,
then before they know it, we're in there!

We've got to tiptoe lightly, ladies,
make sure the way you feel about them,
doesn't get out to their friends, or it'll all end.
Smile small when they're around,
but don't let your smile turn into a frown.
You must remain sexy through it all,
then perhaps one day they'll surprise us and call.

Now, I'm not knocking anyone for having high standards, but frequently, many single sistas do not have their *own* act together, yet they are unable to tolerate even the slightest flaw in a man. This single sista type must first examine herself and get the log out of her *own* eye before trying to get the speck out of someone else's. She obviously does not understand the meaning of love because love looks at the inner, not the outer appearance of things. It would be very difficult for her to find and hold on to a life-mate because the only one that she is willing to accept is the fantasy brotha that she has conjured up in her *own* mind, and let's face it, he is very rare, and most likely, already taken. Once, I was dating this "man" and I asked my mom how she felt about him. She responded, "Well, Jacqueline, by the time a man gets to be around your age [fortyish], if he's still single, he ain't nothin' but a misfit. But you seem to have yourself a nice enough misfit!" (Gee, thanks, Mom!)

On the other hand, however, many single sistas have such low self-worth that they are willing to have *any* man around just for the sake of having a man. So what if he has other women! This single sista does not have enough love for herself to stand up and demand respect.

Number Two Won't Do

I'm not the type of woman
who will settle for being number two
when I come complete enough to be any man's number one.
I won't be used just to fill in all the empty pieces.
I might be single, but I'm not yet done.

You say she doesn't give you what you need.
You say I'm all you'll ever need and more.
If that's the case, why do we have to sneak to be together?
What in the world am I ducking and dodging for?

You tell me all about her as though I'm just a buddy, a pal.
What do you think this does to my heart?
You need to handle your number one without me.
These games you're playing are just pulling us apart.

I'm not saying I'm giving you an ultimatum,
that kind of pressure, I won't put you through.
I've made up my mind for and by myself.
I've decided that for me, number two just won't do.

It does not matter to these sistas if the man has a job, a place, an education, atheistic views, a car, money, a slew of children whom he has abandoned, or a reputation for lying and cheating and beating her until she's black and blue. They feel that they need a man to make them feel complete, so they accept almost anything that comes with having one—even if he means her no good. They are willing to sacrifice their, and their children's, well-being in order to take care of undeserving, dependent, disrespecting single men by giving them money, rides, sex, things, and a roof over their heads. They wash their clothes, cook their meals, accept their lies, allow them to be unfaithful and noncommittal in the relationship, and just about anything else in order to keep them. If you let her tell it, "Any man beats no man."

Unlike the single sistas whose standards are too high, their problem is that they haven't yet established *any* standards for themselves. It would be very difficult for this sista type to secure and maintain a life-mate because she is unable to love a brotha the way he needs to be loved—because she doesn't even know how to love herself, let alone him. How can she give something she doesn't have? Sure, it looks like love. After all, she cooks, cleans, and gives a man everything he wants. But all she is really giving is herself to be used as a doormat to be trampled on and a receptacle to be dumped on and dumped in. She needs to ask herself why she would attract, consider, and even marry such losers.

At one time in my life, I, too, was a single sista who settled just for the sake of having a man around. I had to take a look at myself to figure out why I let myself get so low, and thus, concluded my loneliness had led me down the wrong path.

I Won't Be Misused

I guess I'm just lonely. It seems to me that the only
people around me are the people who have to be.
Everyone else wants to use me up (come pick me up,
loan me some cash, how 'bout some sex,
let me crash at your pad).
I'm tired! It's wearing me out!
Now it's about
living my life for me.
I'm gonna be how I want to be.
People ain't gonna change and I will not rearrange
my life to benefit everyone else.
I'm gonna look out for myself.
I will not be misused, belittled, abused by no one or nothing.
'Cause I cannot stand to feel the way that I feel
when they only say to me,
"Can you? Will you?
Would you? Could you?"
I know it's better to give than to receive,
but it's in my best interest to leave
the moochers alone.
God bless the child who's got his own.

Sometimes as single sistas we ask ourselves, "Why can't I get a man?" We wonder, "Am I too ugly, too fat, too skinny, too intimidating, too self-assured, not intelligent enough?" "Is my hair too short, too fake, too nappy, too what?" Have yawl been out to the clubs lately? It's almost as if you have to advertise what you can offer a man in bed by showing them your cleavage, your thighs, your behind, and how seductively you can move on the dance floor. We women make it easy for men to have low opinions of us, so why should they waste their time or their money on a real woman, when they can get the same "stuff" with fewer demands? A very wise friend of mine once told me, "When the morals of women become as low as some of those triflin' men, then that's when we're all in trouble." Hmm . . . I'm tellin' yawl . . .

There's a Reason

There's a reason men think so little of us:
it's because we think so little of ourselves.
We base our worth on the shape of our behinds,
the length of our hair,
the many ways we get them to stop and to stare.

We brag about being the bomb only because
we know how to move in bed.
We know how to use them to give us money and stuff
to help us to get ahead.

Then when they start to think so little of us,
we have the nerve to wonder why.
We expect to be treated with the utmost respect,
but respect, we cannot buy.

It's something you have to earn, girlfriend,
and something you don't deserve
as long as your legs are gaped open wide
for some disrespecting "perve."

You make it hard on the ones of us who really "got it going on,"
to get any kind of respect.

Instead all we get is disrespect,
and, ultimately, neglect.

But that's all right, we still won't settle;
gonna keep our standards high.
We refuse to throw our values out
just to say we have a guy.

The right one will come along for us
in due season.
When you keep on getting the duds, girlfriend,
remember . . . There's a Reason!

If the single sista expects to have a flourishing relationship, she must first have the love of God in her, then she must love herself, without compromising who she is, and to whom she belongs, for without loving herself and God, she is unable to truly share love with others. If we embrace our position on this earth as Heiresses, or Daughters of the Most High King, and truly understand the power of our Father, then we would not allow ourselves to be a doormat or a receptacle for others.

Lastly, single sistas have to be willing to give love according to the way that God desires for us to love—unfailingly, unconditionally, obediently, patiently, unselfishly, sincerely, deeply, kindly, forgivingly, and without fear. All too often, I hear of women trying to hold on to a man, even though they know for themselves that he is not good to and for them. God speaks to their hearts and shows them negative things that are going on in the relationship, but when they go to their man for confirmation, he denies everything. The sista may have all the evidence in the world, but no guts to move on, so she gives the man she is dating an ultimatum by telling him to either change his doggish ways, or leave. (The truth of the matter is . . . you can leave, too.) He lies and says, "It won't happen again," so the cycle repeats itself. She is left bitter, compromised, and in a state of confusion, hoping that one day he'll change. One day he might change, or perhaps even two days; he might even convince her of his sincerity by having her walk her crazy and disillusioned behind down the aisle like a fool, and say, "I do." Then she has the nerve to wonder why she feels so unloved and is so miserable.

We pray to God for answers. He shows us that there is some sort of unfaithfulness going on—most likely with the finances, other women, or with his lifestyle, yet we are too unfaithful to base our decision to leave a man on what is in our heart and our mind. We rely on a man for permission to get out of the relationship. Our security needs to be in what thus saith the Lord, trusting in what God puts in our hearts and not in that which comes out of the mouth of a man. After all, God told us to put our trust in no man

(Jeremiah 9:4). We are human beings and, as such, we have souls. What good is it for us to have souls if we are not going to acknowledge what the Lord speaks to them? We need to stand firm in the Lord and not accept anything in our lives that is not of Him, if we are going to be the strong, virtuous women that we, as single sistas, can and are expected to be.

Our Single Brothas

Brothas, when I get together with my single sistas, as you are all probably aware, you are a major topic of our conversation. No offense, but it's time for some of us sistas to move on with our own lives ... at least until some of yawl get your acts together, because the way I see it, yawl need some help! Let's keep it real ... relationships between sistas and brothas are in a state of emergency! It's going to take some strong sistas and some strong brothas who are truly bothered by this separation to mend the gap. I'm sure many of yawl have heard the song "Black Brotha" by Angie Stone. When I heard this hit song, I couldn't help but wonder if Angie really meant the positive words that she sang about black men, or whether this was an attempt to get society (or more specifically, black women) to respect them and not judge them by their many negative stereotypes. With all due respect, Angie, I like the beat, and ... and the music, it's really quite melodic, but I know you can't mean that there is no one above the black brotha. That part really disturbs me. What about the Father, Son and Holy Ghost?

Now, I'm not here to bash our single black brothas, but, personally speaking, I just haven't encountered many strong ones. As a female, I recognize the fact that wives are to submit to their husbands, but in order for me to submit, you've got to earn my respect. If I were married, I would love to be able to submit; that would take some of the burden off of me. But I have to be able to look up to a man, admire him, trust him, and respect him. How can I look up to someone whose behavior is beneath me?

Men These Days

My Father told me there'd be days like this;
when men would be lovers of self.
It's a dog-eat-dog world, each out for his own,
don't you dare ask nobody for help.

Can't tell these days the women from men,
most men have gotten so weak.
They keep their true feelings so well concealed.
It's like a game of hide-and-seek.

So eager to run from the first hint of work,
don't they know that's what relationships require?
They'd rather just take the easy way out
and lay up with these "women for hire."

What happened to the wining and the dining these days?
It seems all they want is a roll in the hay.
It doesn't matter who they're rolling with,
that's why so many have gone astray.

Such fragile little boys, so hopeless and scared,
I'm more man than they'll ever be.

Why can't I find a man who's powerful and strong?
Why can't I find a man like me?

As hopeless as the situation appears that single sistas will get to marry an eligible brotha and although the number of couples tying the knot is on a rapid increase, still, only a very small number are going outside of their race, marrying white men or men of other races. Many sistas just can't see themselves giving up on our black brothas, throwing in the towel, and crossing the racial line. For whatever reason(s), despite the daily challenges that our brothas face, many of us single sistas are still hoping that God will send us one of His hidden treasures, a rare jewel, a priceless commodity— a good, strong, loving, eligible, heterosexual, Christian brotha.

Unfortunately, as much as single sistas may want a single brotha, oftentimes we do not appear open to receiving one because we are perceived as being "stuck up."

Don't Assume

You assume I'm stuck up, but you don't know
what's going on inside my head.
I'm just fed up with the games
and all the bull that I've been fed
by members of the opposite sex and that's the reason why
I refuse to even look your way each time you pass me by.

Oh yes, I see you looking at me from the corner of my eyes,
but I don't want to take a chance,
'cause I'm sick of all the lies.
I'm really a very sweet person,
how I wish that you could see,
but each time I reveal my true nature,
someone ends up dogging me.

I have to guard my precious heart;
don't want it broken any more.
This very special soul of mine,
I've come to treasure and adore.
If I don't look out for myself, who else in the world will?
These feelings that I have for myself,
I won't let any one steal.

It took me so long to get to this point of defending myself.
There used to be a time when I put
more stock in everyone else.
So don't assume I'm stuck up just 'cause
I don't look at you and say, "hi."
It just seems to work out better for me
to look away and pass you by.

I can't speak for all sistas, but the things that keep me hoping for a black man are:

- His strong and manly physique
- His suave walk and his laid-back talk
- His ability to turn a woman on with his sexy look, the crack in his smile, his warm, loving hugs, his sensual touch
- His thick, juicy lips
- His ability to kiss and make love ever so passionately and pleasingly
- His plump behind and his thick thighs
- His smooth, sexy bald head
- His creamy brown skin
- And most importantly, his ability to relate to me, respect me, understand me and love me as a black woman

So, with all of us single sistas out there seeking after our diamond in the rough, what are we to do? Obviously I do not have all the answers, because if I did, I suppose I might have a man of my own right now. What I do know, however, is that if we are going to be the righteous women that God has designed us to be, we must first look inside ourselves to ascertain that we are holy and walking in His will according to His purpose for our lives. If we expect to get and keep a good strong black brotha, we can't keep judging them and expecting them to be perfect, especially since we, ourselves, may have some issues that need to be worked out. After all, the Lord has told us that not one of us is righteous (Rom 3:10). Therefore, we must release our image of the "perfect man" and either be willing to accept one as he is or to let him go.

There are some common mistakes that we sistas make that tend to distance our brothas from us, and we should be aware of them, so as not to "scare them off." First of all, we tend to be insensitive to the fact that our brothas are fighting against great odds and that they may have low self-esteem, thus contributing to issues regarding tremendous egos[1]. Therefore, they need to be loved tenderly and gently, with understanding and compassion. Secondly, we some-

---

[1]DeJohng, Monique and Cato-Louis, Cassandra. *How to Marry a Black Man. The Real Deal.* (New York: Doubleday, 1996), 110.

times judge them based on our past with other men, throwing our mistrust of the entire male race up in their faces. If we are unable to trust them based on our experiences with other men, then we should just simply leave them alone until we work out our own trust issues. Thirdly, we sometimes get impatient and "rush things," assuming that the relationship is more serious than it actually is. Oftentimes we assume that because we have given in to our, or his, sexual desires, that this automatically means there is a commitment. We need to learn to relax and just enjoy the dating process, as men seem to be able to do so well.

On the other hand, although the deck is stacked against him, and as desperate as we single sistas can sometimes be to have a man in our lives, it does not give our brothas the right to disrespect, abuse, or misuse us. But how many of us sistas have horror stories to share about things our brothas have done to us and some of the awful ways they've treated us? (and vice versa, I'm sure). However, if we, as brothas and sistas, truly loved one another, and ourselves, then we wouldn't mistreat each other, nor would we allow ourselves to be mistreated *by* others. When we are being mistreated, disrespected, used, and abused, we need to learn how to speak up for ourselves and kick folk to the curb.

I once dated an inconsiderate man, who couldn't seem to catch my subtle hints about not wanting him around me anymore, so I just had to come out and tell him exactly how I felt.

Nothing In It For Me

You're at my house every chance you get,
sitting up under me.
That spot on my couch is wearing out
and starting to fade gradually.

My utility bill that I pay each month
is increasing rapidly.
The extra time I once had for myself
has decreased dramatically.

My children are starting to feel left out
because you're always here.
Every time we have somewhere to go,
you're holding up the rear.
What's really unacceptable is that
you're always drinking beer.
You have the nerve to hoard my remote,
but it's not your TV, dear.

I know you're hungry because I smell your breath
and hear your stomach roar,
but you haven't taken me out to eat once,
so I ain't feeding you no more.

I'm trying not to be rude and tell you to use the door,
But your conversation is so shallow,
and you're really quite a bore.

Where's your home, your job, your pride,
your friends and family?
I thought I could kick it with someone like you
when we met initially,
but "kicking it" is all you care to do,
and I'm just not that lonely.
I've got to shut this madness down;
there ain't nothing in it for me.

If a man (or woman) doesn't want to (or can't) live up to our standards, then, instead of lowering our standards to be with him/her, it is best that we eject him or her from our lives and move on. If our moving on means that we'll be stuck without a mate, even if for our entire lives as, let's face it, some of us will, then we must make the best of our situation and continue living, anyway; looking to the Lord to provide all our needs, as *He* is our husband (Isaiah 54:5). We must go to Him in prayer for all of our decisions that we make, just as a married woman would consult her earthly husband. However, whether we are single or married, we must look to God as our leader, provider, friend, lawyer, doctor, teacher . . . our all in all.

 Just Wait

We've heard, time and time again that we need to just wait on the Lord. From the beginning of time, God has had His plans for our lives already laid out for us (Ephiseans 1:11). Each of us is uniquely designed by Him. He knows our every need and desire, and His desire for us is to lean on Him in all our ways so that He can direct our paths. We need to accept His will for our lives and not go against His grain, so that we may live in perfect peace.

Keep Still

At the end of the day, when I lay down my head,
I wish a man were cuddled up with me in bed.
But for the past few years, it's been obvious to me
that the Lord has something He wants me to see.
He wants me to know how it feels to depend on Him—
to depend on Him, and only Him.

I know that I'm one of His chosen few,
so I want to do just what He wants me to do.
If He wants a man in my life, He'll put one there.
I'm sure if one is to be there, He'll make me aware.
I'm just gonna hang on to God's unchanging hand.
If He wants me to have one, He'll send me a man.

Let's face it though, sistas,
there aren't enough good ones to go around.
Many are gay, on drugs, incarcerated or beneath the ground.
So if God chooses to bless me with one to call my own,
I'll be happy not to have to go to bed alone.
But if I should forever remain single and free,
I know God will continue to provide for my needs.

I only want to walk in accordance with His will,
so I'll continue to wait on Him and keep still.

When we keep our spiritual ears open, we are able to hear His voice as He speaks to us. When Jesus lived on the earth, as He spoke in parables, He said on numerous occasions, "He who has ears, let him hear." It's not enough for us to listen; we have to be obedient to His words and *do* what the Lord tells us to do.

One day when I was a child, I went swimming at a lake with my sister. We decided to venture over to an unsafe area that was clearly marked DO NOT ENTER. A big waterfall that led to a river from the main swimming area was coming down mightily. We decided to put our heads underneath the waterfall to see how strong the water would feel coming down on our heads. The water was falling down so hard that it caused me to lose my balance. I slipped off the slippery rock upon which I was standing and drifted into the unsafe waters of the river, where the current was strong and powerful. Trying to fight against the current to get back to where my sister was standing, I was exhausted and was left with no other choice but to give up my fight. I ended up being tossed alongside the bank of the river, where I was able to grab on to some weeds and managed, through my exhaustion, to pull myself out of the water. I had made it to safety, praise the Lord! Getting back to where my sister stood was a struggle. The weeds were thick, and I feared that snakes and harmful creatures were nestled inside them. Fighting for my breath, I finally approached my sister, and she asked me, "Didn't you hear that lady yelling at you to go with the current?" I told her that I couldn't hear anything except the mighty rush of the waters. We laughed at how ridiculous I looked screaming for my life, when all I had to do was relax and go with the current. We happily went back to the other side of the lake where the water was calm, never to return to the unsafe side again.

Had we not been disobedient in the first place by venturing into unsafe territory, I would have never had to experience such a fearful, life-threatening trauma. Even when I did slip into the strong current and the lady was yelling at me, I was unable to hear her because the current was so fierce and loud. Getting back to safety was a struggle because I was exhausted and afraid of what might have been lying within the weeds. But through it all, God brought me back and kept me safe (even in unsafe territories). I learned from that experience that it is *never* beneficial to go against God's current or outside of the boundaries that He has for us by sinning, being disobedient, and not listening to what He tells us. If we do go against God's current, then it becomes difficult to hear His voice because we distance ourselves from Him. Getting back to safe ground may be a struggle, but we must keep our eyes and ears focused on Him. We must give up the fight and not go against the current, putting every one of our problems into God's hands, if we want Him to take us to safety, where He wants us to be, doing what He wants us to do. If it weren't for a man named Adam, who went outside of the boundaries that God had laid out for him, man would not be in the position that we are in today. But through Christ, God has given us the opportunity to return to safe ground.

We have to just wait on Him and look to Him for direction, walking in the destiny which He has purposed for our lives. If we but wait on Him, our lives will be blessed. Sometimes the wait can seem long and hard because we want it our way. We want what we want, how we want it, when we want it, why we want it, and where we want it. But God has all the answers and only He knows what is best for us. He created us how He wanted us to be, for His glory, and not for our own. Oftentimes we worry when things do not go *our way*, but God has it all under His control. Our battles belong to the Lord. He wants them, and we don't, so why do we try to hold on to them so tightly? Why do we sometimes use Him as a last resort after our own plans fail us and after we have messed everything up? Why don't we just submit to Him in everything we do and go to Him for His approval and blessings at the start of our decision-making? In everything He does, whether it's rewarding us or reprimanding us, He has our best interest at heart—just as parents do their children. We have to believe that! So, just wait!

When I think of that word, "wait," in human terms, there is a negative connotation attached to it. It means that I must be patient, tolerant, willing to put my plans on hold, stand still, become at the mercy of others, and bide my time. This can be quite difficult for a strong type-A personality such as myself—who is used to just getting out there and getting her feet wet by doing. But in a spiritual sense, I am comforted when I can rest my plans and decisions on the shoulders of the Almighty God, knowing that it is only He who sees what is up the street, down the corner, and around the bend. So, like a spoiled brat, as much as I sometimes want it *now*, I know that God has all the answers and I am comforted and at peace only when I wait on Him. When I wait on Him, I know that I am in *His* will, within *His* boundaries, and, therefore, I am on safe ground.

I could be married today, probably literally twenty times over, if I chose to spend my life with men who do not have my best interest at heart and those with whom I know God has not joined me. It is more important to me, however, to have peace in my life. And I know that peace will not rule my life as long as I am going against God's grain. He told me to choose this day whom I will serve, and I have decided to follow Jesus—no turning back . . . no turning back (Joshua 24:15). If I marry or even date a man who does not walk with the Lord, then I have made a foolish decision, and there will be undesirable consequences affecting my decision. But if I choose a God-fearing Christian man who loves me and is good to and for me, one who meets the approval of my Father, then I know that whatever happens in the relationship will work out for the good. For we know that all things work together for the good of those who love the Lord, for those who are called for His purpose (Romans 8:28).

Having been divorced twice, I went against God's grain by marrying men who did not meet with my Father's approval, so I am speaking from experience. All these relationships brought me (with the exception of my two lovely daughters) were heartache and misery. However, I learned some of my most valuable lessons from these mistakes, so, because I am called for my Father's purpose, even these mistakes worked out for the good. Had I not gone through these tests, I would not have this testimony, which means that I would not have had the opportunity to help other single folks with some of their struggles. It was because of these hardships and the lessons that accompanied them that I have made up my mind to just wait on the Lord. Never wanting to make the mistake of yoking myself together with a man who is not good to and for me, I decided to go to the Lord to find out how I would know if I was making yet another mistake. His answer was ever so simple, as I've found that it always is. (So simple, in fact, that you may need to read the following poem twice in order to "get it.")

How Will I Know?

I asked my Lord, "How will I know
who the right man is for me?
There are so many men out there,
but which one could he be?"

I wondered if there was a certain sign or something that gave it
   away.
He answered in His still, small voice,
"When you mean the vows you say."

I guess He told me!

I've heard it said that when you know better, you should do better. Although I knew I was making mistakes in the past by yoking myself together with men who were not worthy of me, still, I continued in that cycle. I had to make a conscious decision to do better, and now, I will only choose to yoke myself with the one man who loves me, and the one who I respect enough to honor the vows that I hope to one day be able to say, with sincerity.

Lord, Let Him Be the One

He's all I ever wanted in a man, and more.
I never met a man quite like him before.
He's so strong on the outside: a man of character and pride,
but on the inside, he's as soft as a dove,
filled with kindness, tenderness, sweetness, and love.
I don't even think he knows
just how much his heart glows.
When we're together, we have so much fun.
Lord, let him be the one.

I've had my share of men in life.
On paper I've even been someone's wife.
I believe he's the one that I've been waiting for;
he's the only man my heart adores.
I jumped the gun
with the other ones.
You forgave me for my past mistakes,
hear me now, dear Lord, for goodness' sake!
As for all the other men, I'm done.
Please Lord, let him be the one.

I've made up my mind not to go against your will
because I want your plans for my life fulfilled.

Tell me Lord, is he the one for me?
Open my eyes so that I can see.
Please, Father God, look after my heart
and protect it from love's fiery darts.
I believe it was you who sent him to me.
Who else could have delivered so perfectly?
Could it be that victory has finally been won?
Oh Lord, I pray . . . let him be the one.

After All

Woman was not placed upon this earth to be alone.
God's purpose for her is to make man's world a happy home.
I've tried to take my purpose in my own hands
and fulfill my will for my life,
but doing things my way only caused unnecessary strife.

He wanted me to wait and depend on Him
and not jump into situations, putting myself out on a limb.
He said He'd be there to take care of my needs;
told me my empty soul, He would surely feed.

He told us not to be unequally yoked,
but I went against the grain, taking it as a joke.
After many disappointments, I decided to give in.
I knew if I kept doing things my way, I just wouldn't win.

I gave up all my trying, but not my hope,
leaning on His love to help me cope.
When we met, I could feel it was in God's plans.
The two of us are walking with Him, hand in hand.

For the first time in my life, love feels so good.
And I knew all along, if I trusted in Him, that it would.

When I began to do things according to His will,
He gave me what I needed because I kept still.

After all this time, here I met you.
And after all this time, you've met me, too.
After all this time, my heart feels anew.
And after all this time, God came through . . . after all.

Tryin' to Do It Right

At one time in my carnal Christian walk, I had no idea that God meant that I, too, should abstain from sex. I felt that sex was something that I just could not and should not have to do without. I figured the Lord understood that, and we had somewhat of an unspoken agreement that I was *going* to fornicate—no ifs, ands, or buts about it! And even if He did expect me to abstain, since I was His child, and He knew me best, He must have known that I could not do without it, and when I fell short, He would forgive me. After all, He was the one who made me and understood my weaknesses and desires in the first place. He said He would take care of all my needs, and that's exactly what I was "letting Him" do.

After some time, however, my guilt began to get the best of me because I had been praying for a husband, and I didn't feel deserving of the Lord sending me a husband when I had already declared so many men as my husband on my own by giving in to my fleshly desires. It was as though I was trying to play God by thinking I was *letting* Him be God only when it benefited me. But the closer I started to walk with Him, the more I realized that He *was* speaking to me, and He *did* expect me to abstain.

Years ago, I had a big "scare" in the midst of my disobedience. I thought I might have become pregnant and I was terrified. But God's grace brought me through. (Thank you, Jesus.) I realized, once again, that it is never beneficial for me to go against God's will, because the consequences were not worth the few minutes of pleasure (and sometimes the lack, thereof). I started to feel uncomfortable with the fact that God was watching me commit sins with some sorry excuse of a man, who meant me no good. Although I wanted to do the right thing and find favor in the eyes of the Lord, wickedness was crouching at my door. It desired to have me, but I had to find a way to master it, instead of allowing it to master me. I had to first confess my sins to the Lord, then believe that He forgave them. Next, I had to (and continue to have to) pray to the Lord to keep me from falling into temptation, for I knew that if I resisted the devil, he would flee from me (James 4:7).

I decided to give it a *try*; mind you, I said, "to give *it* a try," and not *Him*, a try! I was going on my own strength, and not on His. First I went fifteen months without it . . . then fell short; then another 15 months . . . then fell short . . . then ten months . . . then fell short, again. Although I felt bad after having given in each time, overall I thought I was doing pretty good for me, because previous to this, since losing my virginity, I had never gone more than a few months without having sex. But ten months, or even fifteen months wasn't good enough for Him, because He plainly told us not to fornicate.

Our sexual urges can be so strong! It doesn't help when, in our society, everywhere we look, we see "SEX" in movies, music, advertising, books, talk shows, etc. Sex may seem like a cure-all because so many intense, deep, private emotions are released during the act of it. Let's face it . . . sex is very pleasurable and difficult to resist. If you are constantly bombarded with sexual thoughts, it can take your concentration away from your priorities in life and can induce anxiety. Sexual thoughts can cloud our judgment and cause us to wonder who we can call. Sex can put a bandage on our feelings of loneliness and emptiness. It is a strong physical stimulus which provides us with an opportunity for physical exercise, while getting so many of our other needs met—emotionally, mentally, and physically. It's a sin that we can sometimes commit without offending anyone else, especially if both parties are in agreement. If done with consent, it leaves no "victims," or so we tell ourselves. It's so easy for us to fall short in this area, even as Christians, because there is a constant battle going on with ourselves.

Flesh and Spirit

Heavenly Father, I'm coming to you with
contradictory thoughts in my head;
wanting to repent, but fantasizing about
the pleasure I had doing wrong instead.

It's so hard to ask you to forgive me for my sin
when deep in my heart, I can't wait to do it again.

You know about this battle between
flesh and spirit, better than I.
I want to say it won't happen anymore,
but I don't want to lie.

Lord, this urge is so strong and sometimes I'm so weak,
but perfection is something I'll continue to seek.

I can't do anything but fail if left on my own,
but with you, I can do all things, as you have shown.

Give me the desire, dear Lord, to want to do right
and arm me with all I need to fight this fight.

I knew I'd fall short on this Christian journey
which I chose to embark.
Just please don't give up on me;
I'm still pressing toward the mark.

So now, with the Lord's help, no matter what the cost, I'm determined to exercise self-control, flee from sin, and hold on to my stuff.

I Ain't Givin' Up My Stuff

My tires may be goin' down,
but there's a tire shop in town;
I ain't givin' up my stuff.
This mirror's 'sposed to be on my wall,
but it'll just sit 'til I know who to call
without givin' up my stuff.

A man doesn't want to keep getting used,
it makes him start to feel abused.
I can't keep calling all my male friends every time I need
*   something,*
and not be willing to give up nothing.
I'm the type of woman who's just not led
to hold my femininity over any man's head.

So, when my money begins to look funny,
and all my change becomes quite strange,
I'm gonna hang on to my stuff.
Men may beg and plead
'cause they have their needs,
but I'm keepin' all my stuff.

60

God told me not to fornicate,
so I'm goin' to try my best to wait
till He says it's my turn,
'cause it's better to marry than to burn.
He knows exactly what I need;
He's heard me beg. He's heard me plead.

So, when my hormones start to rage,
I'll alter my thoughts, to turn the page,
to help me not give up my stuff.
I'll have to stay in prayer to keep strong
to be in His will where I belong
and not give up my stuff.

As much as I want to please my Lord,
I must admit to have fallen short.
But when I've faltered, when I've swayed,
I've felt bad for having disobeyed.
He understands my struggles, and once again,
God has forgiven all of my sins.
Please Lord, help me hold on to my stuff.

In today's society—both secular and religious—there isn't much talk about abstaining from sex, except for the prevention of sexually transmitted diseases—and even then, the use of condoms is encouraged as an alternative to abstinence. How often do we hear talk about avoiding fornication altogether, simply because the Lord told us to? Many preachers even skim over this topic, trying to avoid the reality of it. In I Corinthians 6:18, Paul tells us through God's word, that we are to flee from fornication because, when we fornicate, we are sinning against our own body, and thus, against the Holy Ghost, which is in us.

There is a nearly universal conviction—or so it appears—that sex is good and that liking it is right: morally right, and a sign of human health.[2] Many of us have already defiled our bodies—the temple of the Holy Ghost—but that does not give us a license to continue in our sinful ways. God said *don't do it*. That ought to be enough. We cannot change the past and de-virginize ourselves; however, we can certainly ask the Lord to forgive us of our mistakes and turn from our sinful ways. As Christians, we should want to do what is pleasing in His sight. I heard it said that women have sex to get intimacy and that men engage in intimacy to get sex. Either way, and for whatever reason, when people, both men and women, have sex outside of marriage, they are fornicating, and all

[2]Dworkin, Andrea. *Intercourse.* (New York: Free Press, 1997), 47.

excuses aside, no matter what your gender or how strong your sex drive or your need for intimacy—trust me, if God meant me to abstain, He meant you, too.

Our Father is all-knowing, and we have to believe that He knew exactly what He was talking about when He told us not to do it. There are various negative consequences that affect us physically, emotionally, and mentally when we fornicate. They include, but certainly are not limited to AIDS, teen pregnancy, STDs, illegitimate births, single-parent households leading to poverty, low self-esteem, etc., but I believe that the spiritual consequences involve much more than we could ever know.

The bottom line to all sinful disobedience is our lack of faith in God. There are many reasons why people choose to fornicate; but ultimately they are trying to fill some need in their lives; perhaps it's a need for intimacy, comfort, money, things . . . or even a need to be loved, wanted, or desired. Whatever the need that causes us to go against God's will and fornicate, He is willing and able to fulfill them; whether He does so by providing us with a decreased sex drive, more strength, self-control, comfort, a friend, a life-mate, love, money, things, engagement in productive activities, greater self-worth, etc.—God's got it. We must assess our true needs and trust that God will fulfill them according to His will. Remember . . . He promised He would fulfill our every need according to His riches in glory, so He has to do what He has promised (Phillippians 4:19).

We know that our flesh is weak, so sometimes we have to take drastic measures in order to hold on to our stuff. If it means that we have to leave men alone for awhile until we can gain the strength necessary to help us to be obedient and not fornicate, then that is what we need to do. We may have to make sure that we are not putting ourselves in positions that make it easy for us to fornicate. For example, don't go anywhere with a man where you will be tempted—especially if you know you're weak in that area. If you know you will not fall short in a restaurant or at the movies or an amusement park or other public places, only go to places like that with a man. You know yourself better than anyone else. You have to be honest with yourself. You know what you can handle and what you cannot. Definitely leave the drugs and alcohol alone, as some of us know from past experiences that our minds are dramatically affected when we use them. Drugs and alcohol have a tendency of making us lose our minds, doing things that we would not ordinarily do, and thinking thoughts that we would not normally think. In short, they give us an excuse, making it easier for us to go ahead and fornicate.

If you invite a man over to your house and turn on some Luther Vandross, turn the lights down low, bring out a bottle of wine, and sit on the couch with him, you know you're just setting yourself up, or layin' yourself down, so don't even go there. If you do put yourself in a situation like that and you can't seem to stop yourself, hightail it on out of there, or kick him out, but by all means, hold on to your stuff. Every time you get tempted, ask the Lord to help you. He always provides a way out. He promised He would; just look for the escape route, but by whatever means necessary, hold on to your stuff.

When the Perm and Weave Ain't Enough

I grew up in a very rural area of Santa Rosa, California—a place where only a few blacks resided, and an even smaller number of single black men. It seemed to me that there was an epidemic of jungle fever going on because most of the brothas had a white woman and/or some mixed children at their side. Rarely did I see a black family, with a mom, dad, and children together. I racked my brain trying to figure out why these brothas preferred white women over their black sistas, and more specifically, over me. My own insecurities told me that the reason I could not get a black man was because I was full-figured. Therefore, I figured that my primary competitors were other fuller-figured white women. I noticed that many of these white women who dated black men were much larger, more impoverished, and not nearly as attractive as I was. Then I knew my weight, looks, and financial status couldn't be a factor for me not being able to get one.

I later thought about my flat behind, which could also have been a deterrent, but after thinking about it, this must have been a plus, because most of the white women had flat behinds, so how could this be a deterrent? I sized myself up against these particular white women, and still, I couldn't figure out what they had that I didn't. It seemed I had much more to offer, so shouldn't black men love me more, I wondered?

Still, because white women had something I didn't have—a black man—they were my competitors. I found myself trying to "enhance" my look so I could be "more qualified" and get a black man. Even though my hair was permed and weaved and the color of my eyes and hair were lightened, none of that was enough because I was still a black woman. I was black on the outside, and even though I tried vainly to change my features, I was still unable to find a black man in my town who wanted me. I finally had to accept that I was a black woman; that was it, and that was all, and there was nothing I could do to change that.

My girlfriend and I were on a mission to find out why these brothas did not want a sista. After all, what did we do to them? Where did we fall short? What was it about us that caused them to look the other way? This really started to wear down my self-esteem.

Where They Belong

There I was, in the prime of my life,
and no one was stud'n me.
Every black man seemed to be taken by a woman
of a race I couldn't be.
I began to think I'd never measure up;
couldn't change the color of my skin.
And even though I was caramel colored,
I still just wasn't "in."

I kept a perm in my hair to make it straight,
thinking I could use this as bait.
When that didn't work, I tried a weave,
just knowing this time I'd surely succeed.

I took it a step further and got colored eyes,
trying to put on a "white girl" disguise.
I lowered my top and raised my skirt
and thought I should learn how to flirt.

But that didn't make them want me for me—
only for parts of my body.
I started to compromise what I was about—
the lovely person I was, I began to doubt.

Their focus was on my outward appearance,
and what I could do for them—
not even caring that inside of me
was a precious, shining gem.
They're not interested in a future wife;
in a righteous heart, they're not impressed,
not in the least concerned with intelligence,
or even with how well you're dressed.

They say they don't want a black woman
because all we do is nag.
It's easier to ignore us and say we must be on the rag.
My nagging means I'm caring,
and that I only want the best,
but their interpretation is that I am just an unwanted pest.

The white woman lets them have their way,
she'll take care of all their needs.
They won't even have to be a man—
just lay there and follow her lead.
If we leave our men alone to go off on their own,
what will happen to our race?
The black child will grow up all confused
because there's no black dad in place.

I'm not trying to be offensive, I just want them to know
that I'm a sister who still loves them
and doesn't want to see them go.
To me, they stand for the epitome of manhood;
I just want them to be strong
so they can be the head, and not the tail, of their black families
where they belong.

To retaliate against our brothas for going against our race, and "selling out" of our heritage, our culture, our very being, we thought we would humorously entertain the thought of getting us a white man, knowing that was not what we really wanted to do. So it became an ongoing joke between us.

Ah Mo Git Me a White Man

Chile, Ah thank Ah mo git me a white man!
Ah can't take these brothas no mo'.
Ah mo have to come up wit a new game plan
'cause the one Ah had ain't workin'—that's fa sho!

Ah know bein' wit a white man ain't no cure-all,
but it can't be no worse than what Ah been gittin'.
Brothas have just been drivin' me up the wall.
Ah'm sick of worryin' and Ah'm tired of frettin'.

At least if Ah try me a white man, it'll be somethin' new.
It'll be like goin' somewhere Ah never been before.
Maybe Ah'll git lucky and find me somebody true.
Perhaps he'll even be someone Ah can trust and adore.

He probably wouldn't mind spendin' money on me either.
He'll most likely be well mannered and treat me like a lady.
Ah won't have to worry about him havin' a job neither.
Ah think we'll be able to communicate
when things git shady.

Ah hope Ah can git wit kissin' smaller lips
and bein' in public wit a man of another race.

When people see us holdin' hands, Ah wonder if they'd trip.
Ah wonder if the two of us would start to feel out of place.

Ah can't concern myself wit how others may feel.
The important thang is, what type of man is he?
And is the love we have for each other real?
And till death do us part, will he be down for me?

After coming to our senses, we decided to try to find out exactly what it was that these brothas saw in white women that drew them to cross the racial line, so we literally interviewed hundreds of them to find out why they preferred white women. We were astonished with their reasons, when we found that:

- They could get more things out of the white women (places to stay, money, the use of their cars, things like that)
- Sistas are too hard on the brothas, nag/demand too much and expect too much out of them (jobs, money, dates, respect, car ownership)
- White women provide them with more kinky sex
- White women can give them half-white and possibly "prettier" babies whose hair is easier to comb
- Brothas are able to control white women easier than they can sistas

- Brothas are that much closer to meeting with the "status quo" when they have a white woman on their arm
- White women more suitably fit the image of how a "beautiful" woman looks (white skin, long hair, and blue, or at least lighter colored eyes, thinner bodies)

We rationalized that their reasons for preferring white women over us actually had little to do with us, but about their own insecurities. I began not to be so angry with them for turning their backs on me as a sista because, when I assessed their superficial reasons for wanting to be with white women, it only made me pity them because it made me see how low their self-esteem really was. They needed all these "things" in a white woman to make them feel like a "real man" due to their insecurities, low self-worth, and humongous egos, which had its origination during the slavery period when they were stripped of their manhood because they were not able to be the providers for and leaders of their families.

After recognizing these insecurities, I realized that I, too, had my preferences for how I wanted my man to look and to be: tall, dark, handsome, gentlemanly, Christian, responsible, intelligent, trustworthy, honest, highly respected by the elders, one who would edify his wife, ambitious, adventuresome, not stuck on having to watch ball games, church-going, young-at-heart, etc., etc., etc. I came to the understanding that each person is entitled to his own preferences (to each his own). If brothas preferred a white woman over me, no matter how shallow and superficial their reasons, then they are certainly entitled to their preferences. I also came to realize that true love sees no color, and accepted the fact that even if these brothas got with white women because they truly loved them, that, too, was fine, and truthfully, out of my control. After all . . . who was I to question anyone's preferences? Again, to each his own. I accepted the fact that since true love sees no color, I shouldn't necessarily be confined to just dating black men just because of the color of their skin, and that it would be all right for me to date and possibly marry outside my race. The truth be told, I'm not interested in all black men, but on the contrary, I have known only a very few who have interested me. Although I would prefer a black brotha, I am only truly interested in a man, regardless of his skin color, who truly loves the Lord, and one who will truly love me for the beautiful person that I am—on the inside and the outside.

Where Is the Love?

Where is the love? What happened to it? Where did it go? What in the world is really going on in our society today? Two of God's most important commandments involve love—first of all, to love God, and secondly, to love one another as we love ourselves (Mark 12:29–31). Satan understands the importance of these two commandments so much that he does everything in his power to lead us to do just the opposite. His desire, most importantly, is for us to hate God, then to hate one another. Some say they love God; however, their love is not evident in the way that they treat others. God wants us to treat one another as we, ourselves, want to be treated, this is often referred to as the "Golden Rule." He doesn't *suggest* that we do so, but He commands it. Society as a whole seems to have turned its back on love.

Satan's Got Us Tongue-Tied

If there were just one thing that God wants us to do,
that would be to love;
first and foremost, to love Him,
our Heavenly Father, from above.
Once that relationship has been secured,
then we're ready to venture out
and find out what loving one another is really all about.

We're supposed to love one another unconditionally
and treat everybody right.
Nowadays, instead of loving one another,
the protocol is to fight.
This world has really beaten up this little innocent,
four-letter word.
It's been crushed, killed, ridiculed, and oftentimes,
never been heard.

When it does slip out from time to time, Satan declares war.
He does all he can to make sure it's not said,
heard or felt anymore.
We're so afraid to say that word for fear
of what others may think.

The use of that one word alone,
could cause a relationship to sink.

So no matter how much our hearts are about
to burst with emotion,
this world of hate and fear keeps our feelings concealed
so we don't get a notion
to be bold and real and speak how we feel
and say those words, "I love you."
Satan's thrilled because he's got us tongue-tied.
Our hearts are hog-tied, too.

What God meant for good, loving relationships, Satan has caused to look bad. Everybody seems to be so afraid to make a commitment.

Make That Move

There aren't many women out there quite like me.
It's just your luck I'm still single and free.
So many men have had to pass me by;
knew they couldn't measure up, so why even try?

Sweetheart, you'd better hurry up and recognize.
Take your heart out of your back pocket and get wise.
I know you've been hurt, and I have too.
But this time, I believe love is smiling on you.

So go ahead, take your time to discover the real me,
but don't let your fears blind you so you can't see.
If you want me, you'd better make that move
or you'll have to miss out, but what will that prove?

Love is a two-way street, I'm not driving alone.
If I have to do that, I'll just be on my own.
If left to be alone all by myself,
I'm sure I'll soon be snatched up by someone else.

I'm giving you fair warning, wouldn't want you to miss out
on discovering what a real woman is all about.

*You'd better come on (don't hold back), make that move,
so we can come together and get on with our groove.*

If we were to love one another the way God wants us to love, people wouldn't go around mistreating others for their own personal gain; men and boys wouldn't talk girls and women out of their stuff, against their will; people wouldn't lie to or deceive one another about being in love; men wouldn't leave women to raise children on their own; folks wouldn't get divorced for reasons other than those permitted by God, or put one another in the many financial, emotional, and mental hardships that they do, or hold lifelong grudges against one another, or take out strong vengeance toward one another.

Perpetrator

I knew before long that you weren't all you portrayed.
I saw potential in you only because
I thought your heart was good;
thinking once you'd become a real man, we'd have it made—
all along knowing deep down inside that I should
move on.

I stuck it out with you through thick and through thin,
never having heard those three words,
"I love you," so much.
I even said, "I do," forsaking all other men.
You thought you had that special touch,
but I'm out.

If it weren't for me, you'd be nothing at all.
I'm the one who taught you how to represent
and talk to "the man";
got your shoulders lifted up and standing tall.
When they told you, "You can't," I told you, "You can
do anything."

You think you've risen far above me
since you got yourself some clout;

letting a little bank account, some cash,
and somebody else's name
on your clothes define who you are,
and what you're all about.
It's a downright shame how small and how lame
you are.

It's time to grow up, little boy!
Get yourself some substance.
Life is short and its true essence is going to pass you by.
Which of us is wearing the pants,
you or I?
(You Perpetrator)

If we would just love the way that God wants us to love, then we wouldn't play games with one another, like the ego game. What's the ego game, you ask? I'm sure you've seen it played time and time again. Perhaps you've even played it yourself—and maybe even won! It's a game people play to make a relationship look like anything but love, and the rules are designed to make the other person feel insignificant.

The Ego Game

This game is geared specifically for those
who suffer from low self-esteem.
It can build up your ego higher
than you can ever possibly dream.
If you play the game right, you'll never be the one
to end up playing the fool.
In order to come out a winner,
you must be willing to play by the rules.
Now, the object is to position yourself as the "sought,"
and not the "seeker."
Whoever slips into the position of "seeker"
is always considered the weaker.
Two players who are developing a relationship
are required for the game.
They may be players of the opposite sex,
but in many cases, they are the same.
Once the two players have met,
only a minimal amount of interest should be shown.
No matter how much you might be impressed,
your cover must never be blown.
If you are the one who is expected to call,
by all means, give it some time.

If the call is long distance, don't stay on too long,
but hold on to your dime.

Always be first to say you must go,
just say you have something to do.
Make it look like your life is fulfilled,
and like everyone's seeking you.
Never be the one to set up the date,
remember . . . you could not care less.
No matter how excited you might be,
in no way can this joy be confessed.
If you really want to lose the game, go ahead;
say those dreaded three words.
But why would you want to go out like that—
ruining the whole thing? How absurd!
When you see that things are not working out,
make sure you're the first to end it.
Under no circumstances are you to suggest
that the two of you should mend it.
Always have an escape route in mind
and make sure you're never locked in.
Keep the mindset that you can take it or leave it,
then you'll always win!

People tend to like this game because it supposedly prevents them from being the one who is set up to get hurt in the relationship.

You Ain't the Only One

You ain't the only one whose heart's been broken.
My past hurts have just gone unspoken.
I've learned from them all that was needed
for me to move on,
by digesting the hurt completely, until it was all gone.

Everyone's been hurt at one time or another.
God wants us to keep on loving and forgiving our brother,
and not hold everyone else responsible for our pain.
In order to grow, we need both sunshine and rain.

So, lay your pride aside and accept that it happened to you.
Look at all Jesus Christ had to go through!
He was perfect, yet that didn't stop hurt from showing up.
He too, had to drink from that bitter cup.

Take all your hurt in, cry, do what you have to do.
In order for your heart to mend,
forgiveness must be the glue.
Ask God to sweeten your heart, and let the hurt be done.
And remember sweetheart . . . you ain't the only one.

Folks need to let go of the head games and . . .

Keep It Real

It makes no sense to play head games and pretend
that you're someone you're not, when in the end
without a doubt, the truth will come out, even without
you telling me what you're all about.

You might as well just keep it real—
don't be afraid to spill the real deal.
If I like you for who you are,
I'll like you whether or not you're up to par.

Just don't fake your funk with me.
Let me see how you're going to be
three months down the road anyway,
then I may know how to deal with you today.

If you're always playing peekaboo,
like you're afraid of revealing yourself to "God knows who,"
then you must have something to hide.
You probably don't like who you are inside.

The sooner I get to know the true you,
the sooner I'll know whether to stay or be through.

Is that why you're keeping yourself concealed?
Afraid I'll be gone because you've been revealed?

Lies and deceit, I won't tolerate.
These two things, I'll always hate.
I'm just laying down the law; telling you how I feel.
If you want to be with me, you've got to keep it real.

Instead of looking out for one another, we look out only for ourselves. Even those of us who try to love others are having a difficult time doing so because of all the misuse and abuse that we get from people as a result of loving them. It's as though we're trapped! Our hearts tell us to love, we want to love . . . even have a strong yearning in our hearts to love, but people have a way of making it so difficult for us to do so. We feel more comfortable not even dealing with people because, every time we do, we end up getting dogged out, hurt, and disrespected. This is just another one of Satan's ploys to separate and divide us, and keep us from loving one another.

So, what are we to do? My best advice: Understand that we are all human and some people can be unreasonable and selfish, but we must never let their transgressions compromise our integrity or cause us to become bitter and disappointed with life.

(I also want to add . . .

"Love one another as the Lord, God has commanded, and people will misuse you, take your kindness for weakness, take you for granted, disrespect you, walk all over you and consider you a fool; love them anyway.")

You see, in the final analysis, it is between you and God; it was never between you and them anyway.

Let's keep it real. As embarrassing as it can feel for us to confess, and as much as some of us may, at times, think we can do without, love is something we all want and need. For some reason, though, it's one of the hardest things to get out of folk. God *is* love. If we put Him before everything else, then love can't help but rule our lives. How can anyone love, except if he has God in him? It is not possible! So before considering any man or any woman for a potential life-mate, make sure, most importantly, that your potential mate's life is being led by the spirit of God, as evident by his or her fruit (love, joy, peace, patience, kindness, goodness, faithfulness, gentleness, and self-control—Galatians 5:22).

Message From the Author

To My Dear Brothers and Sisters (In Christ, I Pray):

Many of us were raised to believe that we need a life's-mate to make us feel complete. I would be the last to argue that without a partner in our lives, we can sometimes experience feelings of loneliness and emptiness. We are all basically looking for the same thing in a relationship—someone to give us love and someone with whom we can share our love. We need to take everything we do very seriously because every decision we make—good or bad—affects our lives, the lives of one another, and most importantly, the lives of our children.

Most of the strife that has come my way has dealt with bad decisions that I made on my own without the Lord's blessings. Many of my setbacks were caused as a result of my yoking myself together with men who were not good to and for me. When I started to look to God for answers, understanding, wisdom, love, patience, direction, and every other perfect thing, my life became much more peaceful.

As I continue to direct my focus on the magnitude of God's love for me, I can't help but praise Him for all His goodness, mercy, and grace. And when I praise Him, I know that everything will work out for the good. Like the strong force of electrical current needed to push water of a fountain up, when the praises go up, then the blessings, like the water from a fountain falling down, just fall down naturally; no effort needed.

The poems contained in this book reflect my personal experiences and are in no way intended to "bash" anyone, but instead, are aimed at giving insight, inspiration, and encouragement. *If the shoe does not fit, just keep a-steppin'.*

I would like to share with you all some of the most valuable lessons that I have learned so far in my walk with Christ, and hope you have learned, or will learn, and will adhere to the same:

- Always have faith that God will work everything out for the best.
- Love the Lord, Our God, with all your heart, your soul, and your might.

- Look to God for the love you need, to both give and to receive.
- Let the peace of the Lord rule your life.
- Learn to love and accept yourself for who you are and for who God has designed you to be, according to His purpose.
- Protect yourself from anything and anyone that will affect you negatively.
- Focus on your inner self, and not on the things of this world, as this is what God sees.
- Treat everybody the way you want to be treated.
- Look beyond the faults of others and see their needs.
- Teach *all* nations and lead them to God, through His Son, Jesus Christ.
- Bless the lives of others when and wherever you are led.
- Keep your ears tuned to God's voice, as He leads and guides you to do that which is consistent with His will.
- Always give God the glory for every one of your trials and triumphs.
- Forgive others for their faults as you confess yours to them.
- Life is short, so enjoy it and don't waste it, but savor its sweetness and be appreciative of it.

May the grace of our Lord and Savior, Jesus Christ, rest, rule, and abide with you all even now and forevermore. And may you experience continual, spiritual growth as you wait upon Him.

In His Name,

Heiress Dr. Jacqueline Lawrence

About the Author

Jacqueline Lawrence was raised in Santa Rosa, California, in a loving home with her mother, father, two sisters, and a brother (later in life, she was blessed with a younger sister, Ms. Meg). She grew up in Community Baptist Church and accepted Jesus Christ as her Savior at a young age. It wasn't until much later in life, after several disappointments, setbacks, and bad decisions, that she actually started walking with the Lord and allowing His Holy Spirit to lead, guide, and direct her life.

Jacqueline has always been very passionate about love—God's love, love of her family and friends, and yes, love of the opposite sex. Although she craved to have a boyfriend even as a young teen, she didn't get her first one until she went away to college, where she majored in business administration (and men) at Tuskegee University, in Alabama. Several boyfriends and two failed marriages later, this Christian single parent shares some of her seemingly insurmountable struggles and experiences with men through her inspirational, "bare-bones," poetic ministry. Once she began to look inside herself to figure out why she was willing to accept such turmoil in her life, and made the decision to turn her life over to God, these struggles and "not always pleasant" experiences became a major contributing factor to her strength. (And we know that all things work together for good to them that love God, to them who are called according to *His* purpose—Romans 8:28.)

Ms. Lawrence currently resides in Vacaville, California, with her two daughters, where she owns and operates residential care facilities for people with developmental disabilities. In her spare time, she enjoys being with her family and friends, attending church services, traveling, shopping, collecting black memorabilia, camping, and writing. She was crowned the Ms. Big, Bold, & Beautiful Queen for the San Francisco Bay Area for the years 2000 and 2001, and won the title of Plus U.S.A. Woman's-Division Three Runner Up, 2002.